AF439226

MEHYRA

SRIJANA SUBBA

Copyright © Srijana Subba
All Rights Reserved.

This book has been self-published with all reasonable efforts taken to make the material error-free by the author. No part of this book shall be used, reproduced in any manner whatsoever without written permission from the author, except in the case of brief quotations embodied in critical articles and reviews.

The Author of this book is solely responsible and liable for its content including but not limited to the views, representations, descriptions, statements, information, opinions and references ["Content"]. The Content of this book shall not constitute or be construed or deemed to reflect the opinion or expression of the Publisher or Editor. Neither the Publisher nor Editor endorse or approve the Content of this book or guarantee the reliability, accuracy or completeness of the Content published herein and do not make any representations or warranties of any kind, express or implied, including but not limited to the implied warranties of merchantability, fitness for a particular purpose. The Publisher and Editor shall not be liable whatsoever for any errors, omissions, whether such errors or omissions result from negligence, accident, or any other cause or claims for loss or damages of any kind, including without limitation, indirect or consequential loss or damage arising out of use, inability to use, or about the reliability, accuracy or sufficiency of the information contained in this book.

Made with ❤ on the Notion Press Platform
www.notionpress.com

Dedicated to Mr. Vikas Jha ,dear friend, well wisher, eminent journalist and an author par excellence who believed that I could run my hand in narratives too.

Contents

Preface

The stories in this book has emerged from a day to day struggle and experience. Being a writer I have taken the liberty to scatter my imagination .

Statutory warning: Some characters in this book are not fictitious, any resemblance to real persons , living or dead is purely intentional.

Introduction

Author Srijana Subba

Srijana Subba happens to be a passionate poet, who loves expressing specially in English. Born to father Phipraj Subba and mother Santosh Mani Subba on 15 December 1980, she lives in Nagri, a lush green small and beautiful tea garden hamlet under the glorious laps of the Queen of Hills Darjeeling. She has completed her B.Sc., M.A. and

B.Ed. She teaches at Pokhriabong Girls' Higher Secondary School, Darjeeling. Her articles, papers have been published in renowned journals and magazines.

She loves travelling to various places to represent Darjeeling hills in various literary events. She was facilitated with Sahitya Akademi authors' travel grant in the year 2014. She participated in a symposium on 'Challenges of Nepali Translation' on September 26, 2014 at Mirik. She attended a seminar on 'Marginalised Languages' in Guwahati University in 2017 as a panelist. She conducted a poetry workshop for English department at Maniben Nanawati College, Mumbai in 2018. She attended the three-day translation workshop on 'Representative Poetry: North-East and Southern Interface' organized by Shabdana (Centre for Translation), Sahitya Akademi, Bangalore on 26-28 December, 2018. She attended All India Indigenous Writers' Festival organized by Sahitya Akademi, New Delhi on 9-10 August, 2019 as a panelist. She attended the first ever Tribal Literature Festival of India organized by Tribal Research Institute, Ranchi, Jharkhand in 2019 as a panelist on 'Mundhum Literature'. She participated in Arunachal Literature Festival as a panelist on the panel titled 'Role of Children's Literature in Nurturing Creativity' in 2019. She participated as a moderator in a panel discussion held in Annual Darjeeling District Book Fair in 2019. She participated in a discussion event on her translation work 'The Forlorn Trees' organized by Sahitya Akademi Webline Literature Series in August 2021. She was featured in Jaipur Writers' Shorts organized by Jaipur Literature Festival in April 2022.

Srijana has published her poetry anthologies 'Fragments' (2011); 'Fossils' (2015); 'Fuchsia Dreams' (2020); travelogue 'Reminiscence of Aizawl' (2014). She has a biography of the Gorkha freedom fighter Captain Dal Bahadur Thapa titled 'The Forgotten Hero: INA Captain Dal Bahadur Thapa (2020) to her credit. She also undertakes the translation projects of Nepali texts into English. 'Pristine Stroke' (Nepali poems of Birbhadra Karkidholi, 2015) and 'The Forlorn Trees' (Sahitya Akademi Award winning Nepali novel Udasin Rukhharoo written by Prem

Pradhan, 2020) are her published translation works. Srijana enthusiastically runs a liberal library solely dedicated to the kids called 'The Book Thief Open Library' at Nagri. Her library was conferred with 'Role Model for Innovative Library Format' award at India Reading Olympiad organized by Food for Thought Foundation in 2020 and was felicitated by United Gorkha Community, India-Hongkong.

Srijana has been felicitated in Myanmar for her special contribution to the literature, whereas, she was felicitated in various parts of India that includes Darjeeling, Siliguri, Manipur, Mizoram, Assam. etc. She was conferred with Rajat Jayanti Vishista

Samman by Bairagi Sangeet Pariwar, Mizoram in 2013. She was also conferred an Honorary Doctorate by Bikramshila Hindi Vidhyapith, Ujjain in 2015.

Email ID: subbasriju@gmail.com

ONE
MEHYRA

Mehyra looked on the mirror. She smiled at her reflection. Today, she must have asked 'Mirror on the wall who is the most beautiful of all?' and the mirror must have replied 'Of course, you Mehyra'. She looked more beautiful in the sea green kurta embellished with silver sequin around the neck line and the hem of the sleeves perfectly paired with her favourite boyfriend jeans.

Mehyra was a fair complexioned woman in her thirty's. She had a black long mane thanks to her Indian roots and hazel nut eyes exactly as her mother who was half Indian. She studied Marine Biology and was working as a research associate in University of Carolina Wilmington. She was the only daughter of Hari Iyer and Melissa Iyer. Her father was neurosurgeon and her mother worked in a hospice.

Alike her parents Mehyra too loved her job. At this age instead of having interest in men she was worried about the deteriorating stage of coral reef.

But, it was different that day after all Mehyra for the first time had agreed to go on a date with her colleague after wrapping work at the lab. She hopped on the stairs at the hallway and glanced at the mirror on the corner and smiled. She thought she looked pretty in this kurta. As she was walking on the pedestrian, a feeble voice from behind grabbed her attention and as soon as she turned around, an old man fell into her arms unconscious. She called 911 and ferried him to the ambulance, her heart which was numb with the shock asked her to accompany him to the hospital and she went.

Hi! Mehyra How was your date? You came early? You didn't go to the pub with him? What did he say? Did he popped the question of marriage?' Melissa fired rounds of questions in one shot. 'Mom! You are ridiculous. I did not meet Mike. I had to rush one stranger to hospital.' Mehyra blurted out and went upstairs to her room and slammed the door.

Weeks passed by and one fine day on her way back home in the evening. She nearly ran over a young woman who suddenly bumped over her car at the middle of nowhere. The sound of screeching brake could be heard loud. Mehyra in her nervous self-yelled at the woman but as the woman turned around scared her more. The woman was bleeding and her eyes swollen black. The woman asked for help and seeing her condition, all Mehyra could do as a responsible citizen was to take her to the nearby hospital. Mehyra found out that the young woman was married to an abusive man who beat her for no reason. Being a hard core feminist she could not resist herself to help her.

The time she reached home everyone was asleep and even though she was tired she looked sheen in that sea green kurta. The spring has given way to autumn, the earth seemed to have its own texture of fall colour; the deciduous forests burnt orange. The crisp mornings and sunny days the perfect time of the year for the 'Wilimingtonians' for outdoor activities,

Mehyra intentionally wore the sea green kurta to break her bestie's superstition. Yes! Rama was her best friend who had warned her not to wear that kurta because every time she wore it she had to meet with unexpected incidents fitting in her schedule.

Mehyra was lying on a beach, her sun kissed skin glowed as the Grecian Goddess as she soaked herself in Sun. 'Aah! nothing, could ruin my perfect day' thought Mehyra as she was gazing the horizon she saw a little head and those small hands moving away on the sea. Her eyes inspected the beach in a wink but everyone seemed too engrossed in their own fun activities. The very next moment Mehyra was at sea reaching those small hands. She was shocked to feel the strength of the calm sea pushing her she fought those voluminous water to save that child. She could hear the whistle and cries on the beach when she handed that little boy to his weeping mother.

Later, that day Mehyra immersed herself into weird thoughts recalling those incidents holding her sea green kurta. She plunged in the attic and searched the box in which it was packed. Mehyra had kept the box as this was special in two ways one it was the last gift that she received from her late Grandmother and two everything was hand crafted even the tag in which it was written Radha's cloth line with a personal touch by the designer in fuchsia colour.

She googled the brand and got the address. Rama, I think you were right about my kurta. I am going to India next week said Mehyra over the phone. , though Rama was heard shouting questionnaire but Mehyra's head was already in India somewhere in Varanasi.

Mehyra boarded the United Airlines Flight from Charlotte Douglas International Airport which was 3 hours drive from her home in Wilmington. She landed at Indira

Gandhi International Airport, New Delhi at terminal 3, a hectic journey which took around eighteen hours. Her head was spinning and the sound of baby crying at every jolt was still ringing in her ears. She passed on the immigration desk and rushed towards terminal 2 .She boarded flight 6E176 to Lal Bahadur Shastri Airport.

Her head was heavy, her leg clamps was bad, due to fatigue she soon fell asleep with mouth open wide giving a damn to the chivalrous culture around , her deep slumber was interrupted by a sweet voice of a pleasant lady 'Ma'am! Please fasten up your seat belt and straighten your seat. Open up the window shield as well, we are soon going to land.' She felt like a naive little girl in front of the airhostess and fixing her posture she prepared herself to land on the spiritual capital of India.

She boarded Ola Cabs to reach Hotel Castillo almost 2.8 km from Dasaswamedh Ghat within forty five minutes she was inquiring at the front desk. 'Ma'am your room is ready'said a smiling doe eyed beauty. She dumped her hand bag on the side table and threw herself on the neatly tucked bed. The room was minimalistic but still exceptionally appealing. The green cushion thrown on the white bedsheet had covers made of Benarasi silk. She thought her travel agent was not only a good looking hunk but well versed in his profession too.

The next day she went on boutique hunting to find Radha's cloth line. She got tired and she missed the autumn vibes back home. In the evening she went to Manikarnika ghat. Manikarnika Ghat is a ghat for cremation approximately three hundred corpse are burnt everyday she had heard from the Manager in Hotel and that was enough for her to visit there because she had a firm belief in karma and thought this ghat was the destination of where karma ends. She was sitting there quietly watching the pyre and the rituals. A young man smiled at her. She found it pretty awkward because she did not know anyone in this part of the country though she had some South Indian connection. The man was waving at her and she waved him back. 'Hi! I am Vivek', he introduced, Many things started playing in her head. It was dusk and she was alone. Her father had warned her of Indian men and brutal rape cases in India. She looked at him carefully. He was almost six feet tall, dark complexioned wearing black rimmed spectacles and with Nikon 750D hanging on his shoulder. He was holding on to his camera as a mother holding her baby caressing it often while talking. He was a photographer by profession who had come to

Varanasi on a project. 'Mehyra' she replied finally.

'Thank God! You are not deaf nor dumb' said the young man and they both laughed. Vivek was a person who not only took photography as a profession rather he perceived photography as an art and he believed in clicking photos which could tell a story.

Later, in the evening Mehyra told Vivek her purpose of coming to Varanasi, 'Oh' I thought I was the only idiot who roamed places in a stint. Jay! Maa Ganga! I am relieved today to have met another idiot on earth!' Seeing them laugh their heart out the chaatwala nearby gazed at them with curious eyes.

The crazy souls became friends in no time. Vivek assured Mehyra to help her in pursuit of the maker of that strange kurta.

They roamed the city having the famous chaat, talking about their passion. They were but two opposite poles one a marine biologist who seemed to have vowed to save the coral reef and the other a photographer whose attitude towards life was no less than a fakir. Vivek insisted her to visit Kashi Labh Mukti Bhawan where people checked in to die. Strange it seems, but according to Hindu belief if one dies in Kashi he would attain salvation or Moksha. At Mukti Bhawan a person is allowed only two weeks to be there.

Vivek introduced her to Mr. Shukla, the Manager of Kashi Labh Mukti Bhawan since forty years. He claimed to have seen around twelve thousand deaths. Mehyra in her queer Hindi mixed with English asked Mr. Shukla as what was his experience on dealing with people who came there to die. Shukla in his Hinglish tone borrowing words from Hindi answered 'Well! Madam I have seen changes in people's behaviour when they leave this place. Many people wanted to resolve their disputes and conflicts before their final adieu after all by understanding death a person has better understanding of life.' Vivek was busy clicking photos with all ears to their colloquy, smiling at the way they were talking about philosophical stuff and thought language is just an art of communication.

'You know I have visited River Ganga in many places, but the energy of the river is strongest at Varanasi. You don't need to take a dip in the river all you need is to sit on its banks and the river will purify your soul' said Vivek looking at the calm Ganga. While Mehyra just nodded for she was already worried about pollution there.

The next day, Vivek called Mehyra and asked her to get ready in fifteen minutes as he was already on his way, to Hotel Castillo.

'Mehyra, I talked with one of my friend here and he told me of this place near Aas Bhairav Mandir this might be the place you are searching' said Vivek excitedly like a small school kid. In no time they were in Plot No. CK 15/78, near Aas Bhairav Mandir. Mehyra's eyes brightened when she saw Radha's cloth line written in fuchsia on the small white colour board tilted on the left side.

The room was no less than a chaos but the vibrancy it had would have attracted anyone on earth. Vivek inquired about the Manager and the young salesman gestured them to a middle aged woman sitting on a gaddhi. Mehyra took out her sea green kurta packed safely from her bag and showed to that woman asking if it was their creation. The woman said 'Madamji! this is from our shop only. You know Varanasi is famous for its Benarasi sarees and stoles is a known fact but this kind of art piece done in sequin is only found in my shop.' Mehyra asked about the craftsman who made it. 'Aah! Madamji though I have many Benarasi weavers but this work is done by one of my weaver who has been working since the time my mother Radha who started this business.

She is old now, she is able to send hardly few pieces a year these days. But there are many beautiful Benarasi works done by my skilled weavers. Do you want to have a look?'asked the woman. 'Oh!I just need to meet that old woman desperately. Please help me reach her as I have travelled all the way from US to meet her,'pleaded Mehyra.

'Ok! Madamji' saying so the woman yelled at her staff 'Oye ! Chhotu yeh Madam log ko woh budi amma ke paas le jao aur jaldi laut aana'. (Chhotu take this Madam to that old woman and return as soon as possible).

They thanked her and left with her staff. He took them behind the temple in through the maze of lanes which is peculiar about Varanasi. At the end of a small lane was a hut, Chhotu left Vivek and Mehyra there. While in US Mehyra imagined of sophisticated designer adorn with big bindi and ravishing dress in a posh area busy working on her designs and there she was in front of a small hut where

Vivek had to stoop to get inside.

In light of the sun that pierced from the only window of the hut they could see a very old woman running threads on a cloth slowly and tears dropping on her wrinkled cheeks. A little girl pretty smart asked Vivek and Mehyra as who were they and what business brought them to their house.

Vivek was about to narrate the purpose of Mehyra's visit to Varanasi, Mehyra gestured him to stop. She told her that Amma's work brought her there. She was impressed by the detailing in her kurta done in sequin, so much that she wanted to meet her in person and thank her.

Amma's blind eyes felt the words and she smiled. In all these years no one had ever talked about my karigari. But, now that my eyes are gone I could hardly earn even for a modest living. I am afraid I won't be able to send my granddaughter to school. Had my son been alive today I would have died peacefully 'told the old woman. Mehyra could hardly sleep, next early morning she called Vivek and together they went to the old woman's place. 'Amma! Do not worry about your little girl Mukta. I will take care of her studies,' said Mehyra handing her few thousands rupees in a white envelope. She said she will send money every month. Mehyra promised to look after little Mukta and the old woman this time wept tears of happiness.

'Vivek! Do you think I did the right thing? 'Of course! Mehyra, you know many come here to this oldest living city to experience the spirituality of our country and return without understanding even a bit of it. But, you came and lived it here. May be! It was your karma that brought you here for the salvation of Amma from her plight' answered Vivek.

The sun was sanguine performing a dance on the far horizon before getting lost somewhere and the two souls were looking silently at the calmness of nature, amidst the chanting of hymns and arti.

TWO
MONALISA

Tulsi was trying to explain the rainbow to himself. His Guruma at school had said that the rainbow is composed of seven colours, but to his dismay he could see only four colours distinctly. He watched it carefully Blue, Green, Yellow, Red and where are the other colours. He looked at the far horizon. He was slowly slipping into the mesmerising view of the just showered far hills. And as he glanced above, he would see elephants approaching and the horse drawing a chariot and on the chariot was the sun. He thought sun must be fat lousy man weaving too much gold. He was just seven years old lad with thousands of imagination in his head. He personified everything on earth, even the natural phenomenon. For instance, he hailed earthquake as a strong man wearing a longoti and standing on one foot beneath the earth balancing it, so whenever his calf itched he would loose balance and the earth shook.

He was a plumpy kid with round eyes and a button nose. He was cute little munchkin loved by all. Alike all, Santoki Guruma too loved him. She would often take him to her home after school. He would proudly follow her carrying her umbrella or some times her green hand bag. Santoki Guruma had no son and Tulsi always imagined that when he grow up he would be her son. Among the students of village Primary School, Tulsi was that privileged one who got every chance to be like the member of Guruma's family. Though, Santoki Guruma seems rude at times but she really had a heart of gold.

Sometimes, Tulsi would spare all his time on Sunday searching medicinal herbs for his diabetic Guruma. Every Monday, he would fondly gift her those herbs carefully packed on a paper. In return, Santoki Guruma would give him ten rupees.

One such Monday, Guruma did not come to school so he went to see her after school. That day Guruma's maid Maiya took him to Guruma's bedroom. He saw his Guruma lying on the bed fragile and withered. He kept the herbs on the side table. He did not want to disturb his beloved Guruma but as he turned around he saw a big poster of a robust person who seemed to be smiling. He found it surprising so he stayed back and waited for his Guruma to open her eyes.

'Oh! You are here', said Santoki Guruma. 'Namaste! Guruma' greeted Tulsi. Guruma was about to say something Tulsi shot the question 'Guruma! Whose picture is this? 'This is Monalisa' answered Guruma. 'Is it a boy or a girl?' questioned Tulsi still gazing at the poster on the wall, Guruma laughed and replied 'You, idiot Monalisa is of course a woman. In fact it is the famous painting of Leonardo Da Vinci.' He noticed only the fact that Monalisa was a woman all the rest went over his head. Santoki Guruma was unable to attend her duty for few more days, but Tulsi never failed to see his favourite teacher. The more he went to meet her the more he was drawn towards the painting on the wall. He would come home and tell his grandmother about Monalisa.

Santoki Guruma was a strict teacher in her Late 50's but anyone around her would feel her vigour that would defy the gravity of old age. She had been a survivor of massive brain haemorrhage. Many of the people at Nagri had thought she would be retarded rest of her life. She would keep herself updated reading regional dailys and would put on a fancy bindi on her temple to cover the scar which was a souvenir of her life saving brain surgery at Peerless Hospital, Kolkata on 1st February 2003 by Dr. Milind and visiting brain surgeon Dr. Jakovowski. She was the symbol of strength and her fighting spirit was an inspiration to one and all. She had many ailments for which she was taking medicines and visiting doctors. On addition to this she was suffering from Diabetes too.

Every weekend, Tulsi would religiously go to the jungle and collect leaves of medicinal plant for his Guruma. He had a firm belief that these leaves helped her to keep fit. But, gradually his Guruma's life was draining out like sand from the fist.

Every Saturday afternoon, Tulsi went to watch 'Chhota Bheem' at his neighbour Anil Mama's home. One day, there was no one except Anil mama. He offered chocolate candy and asked Tulsi to sit on his lap. As he sat down, Anil Mama ran his fingers under his pants and pinched him. Tulsi ran away crying. Anil mama would often act dirty whenever he got chance with Tulsi. One day he heard Guruma giving lecture to class IV girls of his school about good touch and bad touch. She advised or rather ordered them to carry safety pins, and prick the monger whenever they realised a bad touch.

Now, Tulsi was very clear that the act of Anil Mama was a bad touch and this time he was prepared. He took out a small but sharp safety pin from his grandmother's old sweater and pinned it on his sleeve. As usual Anil Mama asked him to sit on his lap and he did so but he was alert and this time when he ran his fingers under his pants he pricked him with the safety pin and ran away. He did not wait for Monday instead he went to Santoki Guruma's home that very day because he felt he had defeated the evil and wanted to share every details of the incident to his Guruma.

'Tulsi what brings you here today? Is everything okay?' asked Guruma seeing Tulsi panting like a little puppy. 'Nothing Guruma I just wanted to see you', said Tulsi. He lied to her because he felt shy to talk about what happened to him since last week.

Guruma offered him some sweets. He felt guilty of telling her a lie. Before he bid her good bye he glanced at the wall and saw Monalisa smile.

Early Monday morning he heard commotion near Santoki Guruma's house. He ran as fast as he could. Guruma was on a stretcher ready to be lifted to the ambulance. Tulsi with all his strength made way through the crowd and handed the regular herbs to his beloved Guruma. After all, it was her who had imbibed in him the will to dream and to be courageous and never to lose hope. Though Guruma's body seemed to have worn out but nothing could deter her iron spirit. She gave errands to Tulsi to fetch her holy beads lying on the side table of her bed room.

He quickly ran to her room and fetched her holy beads as usual he glanced to the painting on the wall and today he saw Monalisa'a face somewhat gloomy.

One, two, three….fifty days and Guruma was still in hospital. The more he missed her , the more he remembered her words and he would open his books and study early to clean the school premises. Santoki Guruma seemed to have succeeded in giving lessons on hygiene to the village kids since three decades.

One afternoon he heard the siren of the ambulance and he ran towards his Guruma's house. He thought Santoki Guruma was finally home but to his utter dismay he saw his dear Guruma's lifeless body being taken out of the ambulance. Guruma's ddaughter were wailing and her husband fainted out. Seeing the sight what a boy of seven years old could do. He became numb and slept that night without having dinner.

The next day at school they had a prayer meeting and the second master declared holiday. Every student and teacher offered khada(silk scarf) to Guruma's body but Tulsi offered her the herbs he thought she might need it in heaven since there were no doctors there.

He marked the date 18th November 2016 on his diary, the day Santoki Guruma left him and to maintain the journal was also taught by Guruma.

On his way back from school he heard noises at Guruma's house. He did not like to go to there, yet he went in. Guruma's daughters and maid were arranging her room. They had thrown the picture of Monalisa out in the corridor.

Tulsi thought of stealing it as the memoir of Guruma but doing so he would only hurt her so he asked her eldest daughter if he could take it. As soon as she nodded he embraced Monalisa and saw her smile.

THREE

A WOMAN WHO HAD FOUR HANDS

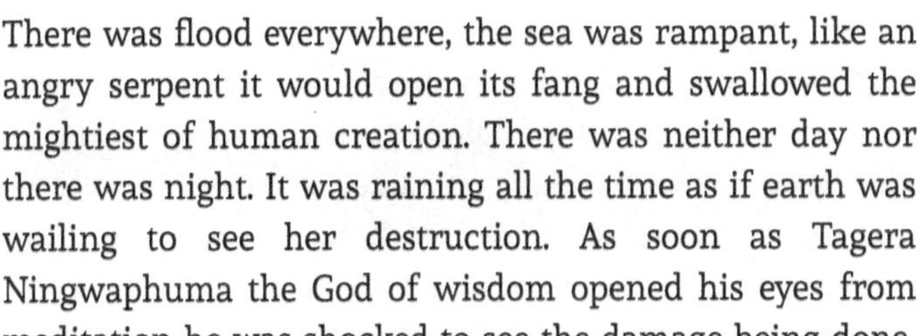

There was flood everywhere, the sea was rampant, like an angry serpent it would open its fang and swallowed the mightiest of human creation. There was neither day nor there was night. It was raining all the time as if earth was wailing to see her destruction. As soon as Tagera Ningwaphuma the God of wisdom opened his eyes from meditation he was shocked to see the damage being done, so he rushed to Porokmi Yambhami the God of creation.

He straight away, went to Porokmi Yambhami's abode. Porokmi Yambhami did not notice Tagera Ningwaphuma. He seemed to be pre occupied with his eyes wide open he was lost as if someone has cast a spell on him. As the God of wisdom Tagera Ningwaphuma approached with his divine eyes he could feel the vacuum inside Parokmi Yambhami's soul. He jolted Porokmi Yambhami to bring back to his sense. Seeing Tagera Ningwaphuma, Porokmi Yambhami fell down to his feet and cried, 'Oh! God of wisdom I failed in your vision to create a perfect universe. I struggled through ages to create this beautiful Earth and I thought I would adorn it with life but my most precious creation human is causing a turmoil on earth by destroying not only nature but themselves too. Please forgive me for failing you. 'Dear Porokmi Yambhami are the creator, the composer of this whole universe and you still possess the capability to restore things you created. So, do not get dishearten. I know you can still create a beautiful soul who would teach the fellow humans the value of life, 'assured Tagera Ningwaphuma.

Porokmi Yambhami created a being. He wanted to make a strong and beautiful soul. He made the frame with bamboo and covered it with mixture of hay and soil. He polished the body with golden dust, and placed the heart from a dove. He made two hands but after thinking a while he added another two just in care for heavier task. He meditated for years and blew the air from Mount Kailasha into that idol and sent it fragilely packed in silver casket. An elderly couple who already had a dozen grown up children got the silver casket while working on the field. They opened the casket excitedly to have found riches instead they were aghast to see a baby girl with four hands.

The husband wanted to kill the baby girl thinking her as evil but the wife stopped him. She told 'Look my dear, our children are already settled in town, leaving us in this village. So, we do not have anyone to look after us since we are getting old? If we raise her like our own she will look after us in our hay days and her two extra hands are just an added bonus with four hands she will do more chores.'

The husband was convinced and they raised her, unlike other children of her age she grew up fast and as expected she had more calibre than others. Her hands were truly an advantage.

She worked as a machine , so she was loved by all in her family. If she failed to help others with cash she would compensate with physical labour.

Not too many seasons passed, she was already a woman. An average looking dusky woman with four fully developed hands. By then, she was already considered heavenly by many , so her parents had to do no hard work in finding her a suitable match.

No wonder soon she was married off to the only educated man in the village. She was happy and afraid at the same time, but her mother convinced her with all the guidelines to become a perfect wife and daughter-in-law. The very first night into her marriage her husband gazed at her hands rather than her face which was adorned with dhungri, bulaki and a red tika on her forehead.

Her hands to him was no less than a specimen in a wax tray for an amateur wannabe scientist. She felt awkward but did not dare to ask him a question as it was not in her mother's guidelines.

One decade has passed in a wink and she was already a mother of a lovely son. She was immersed in her domestic and social duties that she seldom thought as what she really craved her. Even when she had a perfect family she would often find herself aloof.

Her son was the closest but with each passing day her place in his life was occupied by his friends and music. She was lost amongst her loved ones. The festival for her not only was a physical load but a mental torture too. Guests were more interested to discuss about her hands. Some would even go to the length of suggesting her to have only one pair so that she could lead a normal life and she would ponder as what they really mean by saying a normal life. These humiliation as if was not enough her husband would top up with his joke about her and she would just smile.

She would tend to everyone's errand. But these days she was too tired of her life. She prayed to her God all the time, alas her God seemed to be too far. Her sorrow inside suffocated her and she fell ill. She felt a tremendous pain at her back. She would complain about her pain to her husband but he was too busy in his own world. He seldom had time for her. For him marriage was just a part of life and having a four handed wife meant he did not had to worry about his household responsibilities.

She knew deep that her husband did not love her because no man would stoop so low to humiliate his wife addressing her as octopus in front of his relatives and friends. Now, even her son would call her with that name at times.

She cried in her prayers but her God was too far indulged in some other important matter of the world. She often thought of leaving everything and live in the other side of the hills or in the mountains, but by doing so she would only tarter her family's image. She thought of her aged parents.

She was at the brim of suffocation.Had it been for other girls they would have exploded with such an enormous grief being unwanted and ignored the most. She was strong from within so she hanged on even when hope seemed a distant dream.

Her God Porokmi Yambhami suddenly realised her pain so one fine day when she was offering her prayers, she felt the unbearable pain at the back and she crawled, wings sprouted from her back and she finally found her freedom. She looked at the house which was never hers and glanced up to thank her heavenly father, Porokmi.

The very next moment she spread her wings and whirled around her village and flied to the clouds. She chose the most soft and aloof cloud for her residence. Porokomi Yambhami was shocked since he had thought his child would come to him , but later realised the fact that the hardship and cruelty of the ways of world had made her so lonely that in her loneliness she found her world.

Ever since then , she lives in that small cloud which always tries to drift away from the crowd and from there she watches the world.

FOUR

MR.RAMCHARAN SHARMA – THE WRITER

To save her modesty, she raised her sickle and as an avatar of Maa Durga killed Saheb. When police arrived at the scene the sickle was still in her hand and drenched in the cold blood of that Mahisasura, she was laughing hysterically. Hmm with a relaxed tone Ramcharan Sharma led his head back. He was contented with his new novel. He was reading and rereading the climax scene and the protagonist Jagriti who was nonetheless beautiful than Nargis in Mother India in his imagination started flashing as in the Rink Cinema Hall.

'Oi' Ramcharan master won't you sleep? Or at least switch off that bloody light' ordered his better half. Their marriage was an arranged one. She was the only daughter of famous Pandit Kaag Ghusunde who delightedly gave his daughter's hands two decades ago to Master Ramcharan Sharma after all he was the first to break the tradition and instead of pursuing his career as a Purohit performing yagyas, he attained his normal education and became the first primary head teacher in his family.

Ramcharan and his wife were the north pole and the south pole but their deep rooted culture had a great hand in shaping their lives together. They had a healthy son who had a baby skin as soft as butter even in his teens. Ramcharan and his wife argued more often and Ramcharan slowly rescued himself from the clutches of his Mrs. Hitler by drowning in books. He found great solace in books by pouring out his personal, social, political every kind of frustrations in his essays and poems Writing became his favourite pastime.

His one or two articles got published in a daily named Darjeeling Pahad, he was showered with appreciations by family and friends. This gave momentum to his already kindled writer in him and he published his first book, a collection of poetry 'Jaleko Sapana' (Burnt Dreams). Though he could hardly earn a penny from this book, rather he had to pay back the loan from his salary for two years which he borrowed to publish the book and extra Rs. 15000/- for its release function.

Every monsoon the water would seep from the roof top and the sound of every drop it fell on the bucket would mean a pretty good lecture from his wife referring to his expenditure in publishing the book. She would bloat and on the pitch of her voice would go, 'Instead of publishing that bloody shit and giving party to those worn out souls you should have used that loan into proper use by repairing the roofs, you idiot.' He had forgotten long time ago to argue with his wife for he thought arguing with her meant debasing his intellectual figure.

Although, the publication of his book led him into some financial crisis but the recognition he got from it was huge. He was Master Ramcharan Sharma – poet and a writer. He was called to every new book release which happened every weekend. He travelled up to Siliguri, after all he was given an opportunity to read one or two of his poems. The applauds and few words of appreciation from senior and contemporary poets somehow always managed to overlap his petty issues of life for example taxi fares and other expenses when he had to travel to such event just to read one poem at the end of the month.

Ramcharan had gathered a handful of writer friends by then. He heard that the prestigious Sahitya Srijana Award was bestowed only to the best novelist. So, for the last few years he had been writing novels and also published one or two.

Ramcharan's aim was to win the Sahitya Srijana Award because it meant not only the recognition of his writing skill but also the handsome amount along with the award. Even his wife and son were now interested in his writing. At least, the aspiration for Sahitya Srijana Award brought some peace in the family and glued them in one direction. Ramcharan's wife would anticipate in his writing and would laugh often at those soft erotic scenes written by her husband. He had not seen his wife blush except on the day of their marriage. She looked beautiful he thought.

Last year also he missed the award and some Tom, Dick or Harry grabbed the award. Many writers criticized the jury but not Ramcharan after all he had to be in good books if he wanted the award. This year after the publication of his new novel which according to him had been his best till date definitely deserve an award. Since, looking the past few years history of awardee books he was confused at the taste of jury, so he thought before sending it to the publishing house why not find the reader's pulse. After dinner, he took out his manuscript and read out the synopsis of his novel because reading the whole of it meant flaring his wife's anger. His wife intervened him 'No, no, no why don't you write a modern Ramanyana. I mean portray Sita as a strong woman who denies the agni pariksha, you know the passionate love of Ram-Sita their separation and a strong message on women empowerment these all sells now-a-days.' Again, his son interrupted 'Baba why don't you write a new version of Muna-Madan where Muna goes to

Singapore or Dubai to earn instead of Madan. Madan waits for Muna along with his bed ridden mother for two years, but Muna finds a filthy rich man there and Madan also finds his love in Mala Bhauju when they work together in 100 days scheme while making the village pony road. The bare truth sells Baba. The world is practical. To win an award either you have to weave controversy or you have to lobby.'

'What nonsense? What do you know of writing? If I have to rewrite then I will happily write new version of our own great writers of Darjeeling. I would write new version of Accha Rai Rasik's 'Bhudi' or Roop Narayan Sinha's 'Bhramar' . You idiot you are good for nothing. You do not know the fact that art is priceless and writing is a pure form of art. The feeling expressed in aesthetic form in writing when reaches its epitome becomes a classic master piece,' blurted Ramcharan.

'Then, why this fuss? Why do you need opinions? Who is this jury to you? And why the hell you are after Sahitya Srijana Award?' screamed his wife creating a dark silence thereafter.

Ramcharan, kept aside his manuscripts instead brushed his little vedic skills and accompanied his father in law who was old now to perform yagnas. He used the money he loaned to publish his ambitious novel in repairing his house. At least, the coming monsoon he would have a sound sleep with the rhythm of rainfall on his new roof. Perhaps, he would wear his cap of a writer after his retirement.